遇見
【硯香詩集】
To Meet the Origin
in the Future
最初於未來

硯香 著

財團法人｜國家文化藝術｜基金會｜贊助
National Culture and Arts Foundation｜出版

DEDiCATiON

To Shr-Jing（詩京）my daughter who has achieved PhD

in math and Master in physics.

Poetry（詩）is not only foremost in her name

but I wish also in her scholarly life！

Acknowledgements（感謝詞）

I would like to acknowledge Mrs. Bonnie Bailey Chow first of all for the radiance of her smiling face. I happened to see her last winter by the dooryard of Grace Christian Academy where she is the principal.

In chattering, I mentioned that I had newly put my blog on website but as an American probably she might not visit it because it's all in Chinese.

She frowned a little and then turned to a radiant smile which all of a sudden inspired me and I decided to start writing poems in English not only just for her but for many others who might take fancy to read them. I also wish to give thanks to Lolita Chuang（杜杜）, a devoted friend and also a splendid poet herself, Prof. Jih-Chang Lee（李日章）,Prof. Wen-Yu Chiang （江文瑜）, Prof. Yu-Shio Liu（劉毓秀）, Nobel Prize poet laureate candidate K. S. Lee（李魁賢）, Miss Tze-Yi Wang（王慈憶）who worked with NCAF（國藝會）, Miss Vicki Geer, teacher of Grace Christian Academy, my sisters Lorita Hsu and Yen Liu who both live in Canada, my sisters-in-law Chuan-Hua Peng（彭春華）, Violet Hwang（黃麗慈）, my nephew Jeff Wang（王鏡堯）, renowned poets Shao-lien Su（蘇紹連）, Sin-Mu（辛牧）, Sih-hsien Chen（陳思嫻）, my daughter's best friends Shuyan Wu（吳淑妍）, Pei-hsiu Chen（陳佩秀）, Preacher Jasmine Dai（戴惠珍傳道）and Christian brother Yi-Chun Wei（魏益群弟兄）, for their valuable suggestions, opinions and comments kindly expressed to me by e-mails, or through the internet as they visited my website blog from time to time.

For the expertise in planning, editing, compiling and finally the publication of this book, my heart-felt gratitude should be conveyed to Miss Jennifer Hu（胡珮蘭）, Miss Pei-Jung Chen（陳佩蓉）, Miss Lucy Huang（黃姣潔）and Miss Selina Lin（林世玲）who are indeed eminent staff with the Showwe Information Co., Ltd.（秀威資訊科技有限公司）

Above all, I am supremely thankful to our Father in heaven, hallowed be His holy name!

遇見最初於未來

"*Against the Word the unstilled world still whirled*
About the center of the silent Word"

——*T. S. Eliot*

　　原先似乎祇想嘗試用不同於自己的母語的英文語法、思路和節奏，我開始寫一些英文詩，既能在網路自己新設的部落格發表，又看看這樣能否在詩的創作上，找到新的出路和另一番景象。後來，把每首詩先用英文寫好之後，接著就順著原意將它「重新寫」成、而不是「翻譯」成中文，這樣我認為才算是完成了一對「跨語詩」，而沾沾自喜。

　　這不過是分別用兩種語言寫同一首詩，是一種極不同於翻譯的體驗，把文字當成工具的翻譯本身不過是一項技術，講求的是文法以及文章詞彙的信達雅等等問題。而一首詩寫兩次，兩種語言在腦中以各自的方位運轉，經由雙向思考過程，分別各自書寫成詩的形式，使之並行呈現，而完成了一

　　對又一對的跨越兩種語文的「對詩」，使二者之間自然而然產生互相能對照摹擬，這倒是我原先沒有預料到的效果。

　　豈僅如此，細讀精思之餘，我終於發現這樣寫成的「對詩」，兩造之間似建有一座無形的橋，使雙方得以相互闡釋、評比、競爭、甚至還有兩相加持和增輝的作用，的確令我驚訝不止。當我寫跨語詩，就是跨越過兩種不同的語境現實，不斷地來回穿梭，而當我在努力探尋用心摸索的時刻，隱隱然似有一線靈光出現，感到一種神秘的光照，使我覺悟中文和英文這兩種基本上全然迴異的語言，其實是發源自同一個語境現場的總源頭，泉湧外噴而出的。

　　老子道德經第二十五章第一節：「有物渾成，先天地生；寂兮寥兮，獨立而不改，周行而不殆，可以為天下之母。吾不知其名，字之曰道。」我想那在有天有地之前就生出來，「吾不知其名，字之曰道」的東西，不就正是噴湧出各種不同語言的總源頭嗎？

　　而老子的這段說詞和英詩泰斗艾略特的「Against the Word the unstilled world still whirled/ About the center of the silent Word.」兩者其實相輔相成，都是圍繞著「字之曰道」之原理所做的懇切表述。約翰福音的第一句就是 "Before the world was created, the Word already existed. " 聖經中文譯本就把此文翻成「太初有道」。

　　總而言之，英文的小寫「word」是「字」；大寫「Word」就是「道」了，因此老子的「字之曰道」真是寓意深長啊！我甚至覺得我們其實可以從任何一個小字裡面，尋找出至理大道呢。現在，且以「歎債」的「歎」字為例，以我自己的親身經歷說明之：

　　一九五一年除了台澎金馬，整個中國都已經解放了兩年多了，我那精明能幹的母親，就是有辦法一個人扶老攜幼，將男方的老父老母以及四個女兒，一路從湖南長沙護送至香港，買到船票送我們上了駛往基隆港的輪船為止。

　　來台灣沒多久祖父就推我為代表，向那個被兒子休掉了的、在香港有工作的能幹媳婦訴苦，請求她快快寄點錢來接濟應急。

　　祖父對我說：「寫信去給妳媽媽囉；說一切情況都很壞，家中老的老小的小，生活艱苦、危在旦夕……偏偏如今爸爸債務纏身，處境堪憐，積歎的債都還不出，何來這一大家子的養家費！歎債！如今歎這大筆債真是怎麼得了啊！快寫囉！」

　　十歲的我完全可以感受到祖父要向那下堂媳婦求助的急迫無奈，也得知兩年多前卸除軍職夥友做貿易慘敗的父親，如今落得灰頭土臉，差點想要自盡，一了百了！但我的急迫無奈又比祖父更多一重；要寫這封信對我而言有很多難處，祖父要我寫的那些話的字我寫不出來，尤其是歉債的那個「歉」字，我記得在書上讀過，筆劃很多很難寫，我想如果當時問祖父，他一定馬上寫得出，而且還會寫出筆劃較少的那個「欠」字。

　　我就是不問他「歉」這個字的寫法，因為不知怎地我似乎覺得，如今家中遭遇的困難，雖然和這個筆劃又多又複雜的字有關，彷彿全家老小都苦陷在這個難堪又難解的「歉」裡了。但這一切的難題，我十分清楚，絕對不是能把這個字寫得出來就會解決的。

　　要解救全家的生計，祖父託付我要寫這封信，這真的是空前大任啊！而最重要的那個「歉」字怎麼寫呢？怎麼想也想不出，但我還是不放棄，一直不停地揣摩這個字的模樣，就這麼久久地把全部心思集中在這個字上，先是從遠處打量它、然後靠近一點觸碰它、翻攪它、捏弄它、刺破它、穿入它，漸漸地，我發現自己似已穿透、步入了這個繁複難解的

「歉」字最幽深的秘境了。就在此刻似有一片光臨照著我、使我下定決心；一定要跟此時此刻都淪陷在「歉」裡的全家人，一起並肩作戰，有難共赴有苦同當。

雖然我那時候還不確知這個「歉」字到底要怎麼寫，但我卻已經事先透徹地了解了這一個「字」，因為我親身體驗實地經歷了──這一個「字」！

門徒彼得對耶穌說：「夫子，現在就請教我們要怎樣祈禱吧！」

「那你們就這樣禱告吧；」耶穌說：「我們在天上的父，願你的名被稱頌，願你的國降臨，願你的旨意行在地上如同行在天上，我們日用的飲食今日賜給我們，免除我們的歉債，如同我們也免別人歉我們的債，不叫我們遇見試探，救我們脫離兇惡，因為國度、權柄、榮耀全是你的直到永遠阿們。」

有給予的能力是神性，祇有收受的欲望是人性。人生而虧歉了神也虧歉了別的人。人的一生一世總不免時時深陷在「歉」的憂苦之中。「以牙還牙，以眼還眼」的假公私意，祇不過讓人「歉」得更苦更深。這時，慈悲為懷的、有給予能力的神，就送了一件特大的禮物──「兩免」──放在這個「歉」字裡，從此以後，神免了人歉的債；人也免了別人歉的債！

其實「歉」這個字，是兩方（兼）相（欠），但祇稍你一回顧、一轉念，豈不就是誰也不欠誰的兩（兼）免（不欠）了嗎？感謝讚美主！

第一次讀到馬太福音中的那一段主禱文，我已經六十歲，讀它的時候，我似乎又重新感到一片光照，那麼欣然那麼熟悉，原來對我而言，這一段深含至理的經文，不過是在回溯過往，似乎是專程為我解釋，我十歲時剛剛來台灣，就遭遇過並親身經歷過，因而一輩子都難忘的、當年卻怎麼也寫不出的這個「歉」字之中的大道理罷了！

老子將那「吾不知其名」的東西「字之曰道」，換言之，「道」（Word）其實就存在於「字」（word）的裡面，或者循著字的源起，藉由字的光照，也能夠把「道」給找出來。然而，最令人不可思議的弔詭性卻在於；字中的道，是原本最初老早就一直存在那裡的，但我們總必須在繞過奔走過許多路，跌跌撞撞地穿越、歷經過無數大風大浪的歲月之後的未來，才終於能和字中之（大道）驚喜相遇呢。

是故，從字中尋道之道（The way to find Word in

words），總讓我們真的覺得是——To meet the origin in the future（遇見最初於未來）！

附註

　　籌劃這本書的出版前不久，我曾飛往美國賓州，在女兒驅車與陪同之下遊歷各處，但此行最讓我鍾情的還是她所居停的，一座建有顯眼而別緻頂窗（gable）的小巧樓房；典雅、溫靜、端莊。這的確令我感到砰然心動驚喜莫名；記得下飛機後就一路趕車抵達這裡，已經是晚上十一點多了，在那夜深闃靜之中，隔著院落茵草間的一條小徑，玲瓏樓屋就在我前面數步之遙悄然杵立著；此刻萬籟俱寂，夜空悠忽迷離，幽黯冷悄的群巒叢林間，湧動流連的山嵐霧氣，層疊盈漫，屏息以待，似乎正在見證這一場奇妙的相逢！當我定睛向她投以乍然一瞥，竟是如此之似曾相識而為之瞠目結舌；面對這記憶之中從未曾親歷過的情景，卻不可思議地生出一股稠濃的懷舊！以至於覺得此刻她也向我發出惺惺相惜的感應；她一直就這樣默默地，堅守挺立在自己所屬的時空崗位上，期盼著巴望著我，日以繼夜。春去秋來，花開花落，而就在今夜，此時此刻，彷彿終於讓她盼到了，盼到了我們難言的驚喜的「最初」的「遇見」，「於」「未來」的這一天！因此，隔天清晨我特地為她照了張相片，後來就當做本書的封面圖片的主題。這座玲瓏小樓所在的地區名，是沿用早年北美土著印地安人的原始稱呼——「Shamokin」，我想或可把它翻譯成「瞎摸金」，因為在這裡，似乎不論是打從哪兒來的多情有緣人，好像一個不小心都會「瞎摸」到一座黃「金」屋呢！

To Meet the Origin in the Future

"Against the Word the unstilled world still whirled
About the center of the silent Word"

—— *T. S. Eliot*

With the perspective of writing poems which apply different grammar, rhythm and thinking modes of a language other than that of my own mother –tongue, I started to write some poems in English. I not only posted them in my newly founded blog but wished that with such new endeavors perhaps in the art of poetry some innovations could be made.

Then again I tried to "rewrite" rather than "translate" each of these poems into my own Chinese language. I purposely wanted to keep the English language texture and the original contents and style of each poem intact while doing the rewriting. Surprisingly, by venturing in this way, I have succeeded in accomplishing many suites of what I might call them "cross-over-language-poems".

So writing the same poem in two pieces each with a different language is quite an expediction, a totally different experience from doing translation that applies language as a tool, being concerned mainly with grammar, diction, manner and rhetoric of expressions and so on. But writing the same poem in two units each in separate languages, the brain must function bilaterally considering that every language has its own mode of thinking and unique way of expressions. Therefore, with a view to accomplish poems in two- language-suite through elaborated brain exercises, that it eventually could result in the contrast, comparison and assimilation between languages is really something far beyond my expectation.

It further occurred to me that between two poems of each "suite", there is an invisible bridge that serves as mutual interpretation, criticizing and contesting that could further enrich and enlighten the art of poetry of both sides. So this is indeed such a great reward for my small effort!

When I concentrated in working and ruminating in the two languages, I often felt as though I was wandering back and forth between two different language realities, such that at moments a radiance shone on me which let me sense that the well-spring of reality from which those two fundamentally different languages arise was the same.

Tao-Teh-Jing by Laotse, Chapter 25, Verse 1: "Something had been unconsciously made before the sky and earth were born; Seemly motionless and silent, but it has been independent and unchanging, circulating and unyielding, that being so reliable and steadfast as the mother of the earth. I have not yet found its name, therefore I just give it the word Tao". If we dare to imagine, could that something "I have not yet found its name, therefore I just word it Tao" that existed before the start of earth and sky, be the same thing as the well-spring of reality from which arise all fundamentally different languages of all human beings?

It seems to me that this metaphysical passage by Laotse in Tao-Teh-Jing carries close resemblance with a stanza of a poem by T. S. Eliot: "Against the Word the unstilled world still whirled

/ About the center of the silent Word". Both seem to be inspired and generated from the word "Tao" of Laotse. And both remind us of the the first verse of John in the Scripture: "Before the world was created, the Word already existed. " In the Chinese version of the Bible, this verse is simply translated as "There is Tao in the very beginning" （太初有道）.

Accordingly, "word" in small initial letter means 「字 （tse）」 in Chinese, while "Word" in capital initial letter means 「道（Tao）」. So the relation between word and Tao becomes the more fascinating and thought-provoking the more we study the philosophy of Laotse. As far as myself is concerned, I observed that some great wisdom could be found in a small word in Chinese. So herewith allow me to give a " witness" by providing a story of my early experiences in life when I happened to encounter a word 「欠」, which means "in debt" in English:

In 1951 the whole Chinese mainland had been liberated by Communist regime for over two years except Taiwan and the surrounding small scattering islands and areas. Fortunately my mother, being capable and shrewd, overcame all difficulties and hardships, and she managed in one way or another and brought her ex-husband's parents and four children to Hong Kong, traveling all the way from Changsa of Hunan Province. Then with ways and means she succeeded in getting the tickets and saw us all off at the dockyard of the ship bound for Keelung, Taiwan.

Soon after we arrived in Taiwan, my grandfather chose me as the delegate to ask for help from his son's ex-wife who at least by this time had a regular income since holding down a job in Hong Kong. Grandfather said to me: "Now write a letter to your mother, that she might understand what hardship and misery the whole family is now experiencing, being stuck in Taiwan. Tell your mother that your father is now over burdened with big debts. How can he feed such a large family when he is himself ensnared in debts?"

"Debts! with such a great burden of debt how can we all go on living? So write to her, quick!" I was ten years old and perfectly understood how desperately my grandfather was trying to seek help from the ex-wife of his son. Having retreated from his military position two years previously, my father soon suffered a great failure in doing business with his friends. We were even told that he became so frustrated and despondent that he simply wished to end his life by committing suicide!

But at this moment my feeling of helplessness and desperation seemed no less than that of my grandfather; because I had my difficulties in writing such a letter. I didn't know how to write some of the words and phrases my grandfather asked of me to write. Particularly the word 「歉」 which is simply a phrase "in debt" in English. As far as I could remember from the classroom, the strokes of this word seemed very complicated and I just couldn't make it. But at least I could then just ask my grandfather to write down the difficult word for me to copy and he might as well show me a simplified form of the same word as 「欠」, which is by far easier to write.

Nevertheless, I stubbornly insisted upon not asking him at that time. I could so surely sense that the hardships our family went through were related to that difficult word with complicated strokes. So we are all together now helplessly ensnared in this hard and miserable character 「歉」. But what seemed crystal clear in my mind was that all the problems and hardships could never be solved and removed by just writing the word down on the paper.

What an important role and a mission assigned to me when my grandfather bade me to write that letter! Right now the ways and means of living of the whole family seemed to depend and hinge upon my letter. I blamed myself so much that I couldn't fulfill my obligations, only because of the fatal word 「歉」 which I knew not how to write.

Though discouraged and depressed, I decided some how not to give up. I started to focus my mind on the outward appearance of this word as far as I could remember. Trying elaborately to figure it out from distance, then to draw nearer and nearer, then come to touch by stirring it, squeezing it, breaking and piercing through it. Then when I seemed to have succeeded in making a way to the very innermost of this word, I found myself successfully drawn into the mysterious center core of this word despite that it was so hard and complicated!

A certain radiance shone upon me at that very instance,

then I made up my mind and said to myself that from now on, no matter what happened I would stand firmly and unyieldingly on guard with the whole family against any hardships, miseries and calamities to come.

Even before knowing how to write the word, I gained a thorough understanding of its meaning as I ventured to take pains and experiences all by myself the cruel reality in this heart-breaking word——「歉」.

Jesus said to His disciples: "God already knows what you need before you ask him. This, then, is how you should pray; Our father in heaven, may Your name be honoured, may your kingdom come, may Your will be done on earth as it is in heaven. Give us today our daily bread. Forgive us our debts, as we also have given our debtors, ..."

Divinity is the power to give and humanity is the desire to receive. As human beings, we all are born in deep debt with God as well as with other people. From time to time our lives seem inevitably to have fallen into the miseries of debtors. The so-called "Eye for an eye and tooth for a tooth" is but false justice out of selfishness, that could end up into even harsher and deeper in-debted pitfalls for us. Fortunately, the God who is so benevolent, gracious and merciful that He managed to put an enormous present——"both forgiven" —— into the word 「歉」. So from now on, God has forgiven the debts of people as people have forgiven debts of other people!

Looking into the word 「歉」, we evidently can find 「兼」 as "both" and 「欠」 as "owing". If with a spark of reflection and a blink of imagination, "both owing" means no other than "neither owing" which can finally lead to "both forgiven" in the prayer that Jesus taught us.

But I was already 60 yrs old when I happened to read the prayer of Jesus for the first time. Once more just as 50 years ago, I could feel some radiance delightful and familiar shone upon me especially when I read "Forgive our debts as we have already forgiven our debtors"; So I realized the valuable messages revealed in the prayer of Jesus seemed now to serve purposely a perfect explication for me of the word which had been too difficult and complicated to understand and assimilate as a

10-year-old.

That "something" that Laotse had not known how to name, he nevertheless worded it as "Tao". As we mentioned before, "Tao" is the same as or at least resembles "Word" as referred to the first verse of John of the Bible. If Tao or Word is not to be found directly in the word, then reinforced by my own experiences, I am confident that it will definitely be found in one way or another, through the original power, light and glow every word or phrase innately transpires.

As ancient as history of human languages, Tao or Word seemed to have probably long existed in each particular word. Paradoxically, we could hardly find and make the surprising encounter with Word in words until long after having gone through a series of ups and downs of events and experiences in our Multifarious careers have long taken us. I, therefore, would like to conclude perhaps somewhat rashly that the way to find Word in words may be perceived as to meet the origin in the time future.

contents

輯三 沉默和語言 Part 3 Silence and Language

輯四　遇見最初於未來 Part 4 To Meet the Origin in the Future

輯一　風和語言

Part 1 Wind and Language

Mother Tongue of the Wind

Licking up every corner of the wilderness

Piercing through the broken windows

Slamming the loosely hinged doors

Sweeping the dead leaves and dust from end

To end of the streets full of sound and fury

The tongue of the wind swirling and grumbling

In such an agitation that make no more sense than

Resounding exaggeration with no explications at all

In its saying

Such saying of the wind

Smote and slew all his children

Destroyed all his flocks and properties overnight

Brought sores to his whole body from tip to toe

So perhaps then only Job could hear the Word

And accessed face to face encounter with Jehovah

From the swirling and furious eye of great mystery

Where mother tongue of the wind sprouting

That strictly forbidden is understanding

That The impossibility is explication

風的母語

舔盡荒叢野地的每個角落
舔穿破損的玻離窗
舔撞絞鍊鬆動了的門
舔遍街路上的灰塵和敗葉
從這頭到那頭充滿聲音與忿怒

風的舌頭就這樣翻攪著騷響個不停
他心亂如麻他總是在胡言亂語
他總是口氣特粗聲量其大
到底要說什麼他絕不解釋

風的胡言亂語就這樣擊斃人的孩子們
又滅絕他一切的牲口損毀他所有的財產
這一陣風還使他長滿毒瘡自頭頂到腳底
正因如此或許惟有約伯得以聽聞得道

惟有約伯能和耶和華面面相覷
自那忿然掃來一陣旋風眼的神秘中央
而風的母語就是從這裡噴湧出來
祇是你想要聽懂是絕對被禁止的
祇是你想要解釋是絕無可能的

 *Suite Two*

Step-Mother's Face of Spring

——to T.S.Eliot

April is the cruelest month, breeding

Lilacs out of the dead land, mixing

Memory and desire, stirring

Dull roots with Spring rain

With the Passion April seemed cruel but

Less than the step-mother's face of Spring

Which tend to change in notorious stirring ways

Mixing rain or shine with cloudy and gloomy days

Despite a fair lady being a dull dull root

Sings again and again the rain in Spain

Stays mainly in the plain in the plain

Stirring Passion then sprout resurrection

春天後母面

——致贈詩人艾略特

四月是最殘忍的時節

從荒地裡生長出了紫丁香混雜著

回憶和欲望激發頑冥不靈的根

以清明時節春雨的紛紛

也許受難日的緣故四月殘酷

但還不如春天後母的臉殘酷

她總是翻臉又翻臉一變再變

不論晴天雨天總搞成雲霧迷濛的陰陽天

倒有一位好女人雖也像頑冥不靈的根

她愛唱啊唱著西班牙的雨

多半不是落在高原就是降在平原

降在受難之日的荒地

第三天冒出復活的基督

Fill Your Glass to the Brim

——To Emily Dickinson

All you need is a drop or a crumb

That you and birds shared in Nature

But Mystery graciously fill your glass

You said your eyes like sherry in glass

Left over by guests who come and go

And politely saying to see you Sometime

In your diction Sometime means Notime

Secluded in White sustenance of Amherst

Notime could see you Sometime with

You There I Here between the door ajar

Where the oceans and prayers are

Only Mystery fill your glass to the brim

With thousands of poems we are so sure

The Plenty would hurt you no more

福杯滿溢

——獻給愛蜜麗狄金生

妳所需的不過是大自然的一滴水

一粒屑讓小鳥和妳一起分享

那神祕者卻慷慨地要注滿妳的酒杯

妳說妳的眼睛像客人走後

殘留在杯中的雪莉酒

客人來來去去說何時再來

妳想何時來就等於再也不來

離群索居在安默斯特純白的時光

無時無刻不論何時沒有妳的身影

妳在那裡我在這裡相隔著虛掩的門

相隔著的卻是無盡的海洋和祈禱悠悠
唯有那神祕者的傾注使妳福杯滿溢
注滿以成千的詩篇我們非常確定
妳不再被這樣的充盈豐盛而刺傷

Where Word Is Missing

——To Tutu

(What a peculiar name for a poet that it means short skirt
for ballerina in French and grandmother in Hawaiian !)

Where Word is missing, there's nothing no name no fame

If there's no name no fame, there's nothing and no game

If there's no game, there's not even a runner

If there's not even a runner, there's no winner

If there's no winner, there's no one called Savior

If there's no one called Savior, there's only destroyer

If there's only destroyer, to death is life condemned

To death is life condemned everlasting

So there's no game no fame no name and nothing

Absolutely nothing where Word is missing

如果沒有神之道

──給詩人杜杜

（一個多麼奇特的名字，因為法文的芭蕾舞短裙和
夏威夷語的祖母都叫做Tutu！）

如果沒有神之道，就一無所有無美名亦無人之名

如果沒有美名亦無人之名，就一無所有沒有競賽

如果沒有競賽，就沒有參賽者

如果沒有參賽者，就沒有一個得勝主

如果沒有一個得勝主，就沒有救世主

如果沒有救世主，就祇有毀滅者

如果祇有毀滅者，就祇有永劫不復的死亡

如果祇有死亡的永劫不復，就無競賽

無美名無人之名　絕對一無所有

絕對一無所有如果沒有神之道

Real and Sound Word being Found

Soundless mosquitoes make no difference

With mosquitoes making sound

But mosquitoes bites last year means something

Else other than there have been mosquitoes

Humming around

In the whirlwind of restlessness during a night sleepless

Just endure and don't you worry and be happy

Not that the whirlwind would soon come to the end

But the strong the endurance the weak the restlessness

The stronger the endurance the nearer the core of truth

In the very center of whirlwind of a restless sleepless night

You will finally find the rest so real and asleep so sound

As in the wordlessness a real and sound

Word being found

找回深沉大言

不發出聲音的蚊子
和發出聲音的蚊子並無二致
但去年曾被蚊子咬過
和有蚊子一直在嗡嗡叫個不停
卻完全是兩碼子事

在心煩意亂旋風橫掃的無眠夜
你最好要儘力含忍莫擔心要開心
橫掃的旋風我們不期待它自生自滅
耐心越強心煩意亂的旋風就越弱

耐得越久你距離真理的核心就越近
在那無眠夜心煩意亂橫掃旋風的最中央
你終究能找到真正的心安和香甜的安眠
就像終究在無言之中
找回了深沉大言

Indian Laurel Fig

In the morning

I walked by and looked up at the tree

A handsome branch seemed to make pass at me

Seven birds hidden deep in the tree giggling

How enormous and junior appeared the one

But so small and senior seemed the other

In the evening

Seven maid-servants chattering fervently under the tree

After they have taken out the garbage of their masters' houses

No body around but only the tree understood what they talked

Perhaps the ancestor of the laurel fig tree had been an Indian

And so those maid-servants seemed to speak in Indonesian

As I understood what the seven birds giggled in the morning

So the tree knew what the seven maids talked in the evening

The tree could never remember their faces neither did I recognize

The birds that hidden away in the thick dark- green leaves

But only the tree and I now living in the earth bear witness

Of the birds in the tree and the maid-servants under the tree

Both their number being seven in heaven

大榕樹

早晨的時候

我在樹下走過望著樹上

一根俊美的枝幹伸出向我調情

七隻小鳥躲在樹蔭咯咯咯咯地竊笑

一個多麼高大龐然看來年少

而一個卻多麼矮小看來年紀不小

傍晚的時候

七個女佣在樹下交談談得也真熱鬧

她們剛剛才清理主人家的垃圾拿去倒掉

除了榕樹沒有路人能懂她們談得莫名其妙

或許是因為榕樹的祖先是一名印度人
而那七個女佣說的好像是一種印尼文

就像我能了解早上的鳥兒為何咯咯咯咯竊笑
印度月桂榕也懂得傍晚的女佣們在談的事很重要
榕樹也許根本記不住她們的臉就像
我看不到深藏在樹上濃蔭裡的鳥
但卻祇有還活著的榕樹和我能夠為
樹上的鳥以及樹下的女佣將來在天堂作
見證　而且上上下下都是七個剛巧不巧

Snake Speaks English in Fire

As a bilingual shepherd

He understand his sheep's English

As well as his buffalo's Chinese

He would worry and miss one of his sheep

Lost until found as much as any of his Chinese

Speaking buffalo going astray

As a bilingual tongue

Snake speaks English in fire

Dragon speaks Chinese in wind

So eat it and you'll be as wise as God

Says the snake

Says the dragon

We are all but the descendents of dragon

Means the same as the well-spring mouth of wind

And fire sprout from the same one

Tongue bilingual

蛇在火中說英語

既是雙語的牧者
祂懂羔羊的英文
也懂水牛的漢語
一條水牛走失就像
祂的一隻羔羊迷路
最後若不能找回
祂都一樣憂心如焚

既有會說雙語的舌
蛇在火中說英語
龍從風中說漢文

你吃吧你會像祂一樣的
聰明又厲害　蛇說

龍說
我們都是龍的傳人
意思其實都一樣
風火本同源　迸發自同一張嘴裡的
會說雙語的一隻舌頭

輯二　祈禱和語言

Part 2 Prayer and Language

Prayer Without Words

Ants parading in silence of words and

Chirrups sounding wordlessly in words

Oh Lord teach us how to pray

What to say and saying being approaching

Reaching and touching and catching

Don't be afraid of hearing a word hurt

Says Lord word wouldn't hurt what hurt

Being wordless hurt with no seemingly seam

So just say forgive us our debts just as

We've forgiven our debtors

But I fell helplessly in the wordless all the same

As word existed even before the world was made

Before everything how could I utter a word when

I found I live in word and word lives in me

So pray that I say prayer without words to Thee

無言的禱告

在無言中螞蟻靜默地遊行
在無言中小鳥啾啾地鳴叫
主啊請告訴我們如何禱告
我們要說什麼說什麼不過是
想趨近你找到你觸摸你抓牢你

不要害怕聽到中傷的言語
主祂說語言不會中傷中傷的是
無言的中無跡可尋的傷
所以要禱告說求你免我們的債
如同我們免了別人的債

無可救藥我還是跌入了無言中
祇因為遠在造物之前就有了言
老早知道自己根本就是住在言
言也住在自己的裡面叫我如何吐出
一言所以也請垂聽我的禱告雖無一言

If There were No Resurrection

"You fool! When you sow a seed in the ground, it does not sprout to life unless it dies."

——1 Corinthians 15:36

When the last trumpet sounds and as quickly as the blinking of an eye
What is mortal will be changed to what is immortal and never die

That Christ died for our sins as written in the Scripture
That he was buried and that he was raised to life three days later

But if there were no resurrection of the Christ Jesus
The word noon of the second day would have been missing

Neither be there time for afternoon and evening to spend

The night would not only the darkest but also the longest

It would sink so deep that never bottom out dawning

And sprouting into the fatal first thing early next morning

When Jesus should have appeared to Mary Magdalene

By the entrance of the empty tomb with only linen wrappings lying

But she thought He was the GARDENER that should have known

The where-abouts of the mortal body of the WORD RESURRECTION

如果沒有基督復活

「無知的人哪，你所種的，若不死就不能生。」

——哥林多前書十五章三十六節

當最後的號角響起然後就在一眨眼的剎那
凡會朽壞必死的將變成永不朽壞永不死滅

正如經上所載耶穌基督為擔負我們的罪而死
他死了下葬了之後的第三天他卻復活了

然而如果沒有基督復活這回事
他死後的第二天就沒有了正午一詞

也就沒有下午和傍晚的時刻可供你消磨
這一天的夜晚不但黑暗而且深不見底的幽長

沒完沒了似的怎麼怎麼也捱不到天亮
捱不到那天清晨終於會發生的一件事

那就是耶穌將要顯現在抹大拉馬利亞的面前
就在僅留下一堆細麻裹屍布的墓穴的出口

但她還以為他祇是墓地園丁想必會知道
基督復活本尊的必朽必死的肉身的下落

Mysterious Sower

Scattering seed in the field

And some of it fell along the path

And the birds came and ate it up

The sower in the famous painting looks

Like scarecrow and as mysterious as

In the words of the Scripture

The birds in the Scripture hovered over the sower

Mysterious look like swarm of dark clouds

In the famous painting

Birds are not devil and came and feed the corn seed

Because they simply become hungry not because corn

Seed meant Word of God and so hate and it devoured

Birds are so clever that they make nests in the branches of

The biggest of all trees so when they saw a mustard seed

They chose not to eat it although it's the smallest of all seeds

神秘的撒種者

撒種於田間

有些種子掉落在田埂上

鳥兒飛過來就將它啄去吃掉了

在名畫中的撒種者

畫得像稻草人似乎神秘兮兮的

在聖經的章句裡

而聖經裡縈繞在撒種者頭上的

鳥群卻畫得像密佈的烏雲

在那一幅名畫裡

但鳥群並非魔鬼它們飛來把穀種吃掉

祇是因為它們肚子餓了

可不是因為穀種是神的話才憤而噬之

聰明的鳥要在最大最大的芥菜的樹枝上築巢

看見有人撒了一粒芥菜種子在那裡它卻不啄食

倒不是嫌棄那是最小最小的一粒種子

The Vacancy in the Painting

What a rejoice if

I could just sit down with

Him under the permanent shade of

Of a tree in the painting

Now that he is dead

The empty chair under the tree

Is lasting as the cool shade of fine

Tree is enduring as the length of death is permanently

Stretching and stretching in the painting

While in social reality

Some chair's vacancy

Tend to be fulfilled eventually

By somebody that if somebody other than

Him is a chair meaninglessly vacant in the painting

畫中的職缺

永在的樹蔭之下
倘若能和他一起並坐
該是多麼歡欣快樂
在一幅畫裡

如今他既然已死
空椅常在總是一直虛懸
樹蔭長存總也那麼清涼美好
死亡卻一直一直拖得很長不見盡頭
在一幅畫裡

在社會的現實裡

倘若有個職缺待補

遲早就有某個傢伙來補

但除了他以外的某個傢伙

不過是空椅上的尸位素餐

在一幅畫裡

You are What You Sing

When you eat

Don't you bother about cleansing

You are not what you eat

You are what you say and speak

And write and e-mail and what you've made

In a Song

When you sing

Don't you bother about cleansing

For your soul will be washed clean

As snow white and soft and you'll soon

Turn into what you've sung

In a Song

What you sing

Don't you bother about cleansing

No sooner have you begun to sing than

Words and rhythm of divinity and beauty

Make you are what you sing

In a Song

你是你所歌唱的

你吃什麼
請不必在乎潔不潔淨
你不是你所吃的
你是你所說的所講的所寫的
所電子郵寄的所創作所表現的
在一首歌裡

唱歌的時候
請不必在乎潔不潔淨
你的心靈將會洗淨得像

雪一樣又白又柔軟
你自己也變成你所唱頌的
在一首歌裡

你唱什麼
請不必在乎潔不潔淨
你一旦開始歌唱
聖靈就會發出旨意和美韻
終於造就你成為你所唱頌的
在一首歌裡

Repeat · Repent

Toss a blanket from the bed and lay upon my back
As browser senses start elaborately to catch and clutch
Something meaningful, intelligent and probably entertaining
Just perhaps to alleviate a sense of guilt for transgressions
Helplessly repeat again and again

While a little unusual bustles of household things annoy
Just as much the usual bustles of day to day living
Repeat listlessly again and again
But from the tall Yulan tree tops away off the window
An unusual rustling of leaves overheard made me overjoyed
When they repeat mysteriously again and again

Remind me of John the Baptist shouting Repent

In the wilderness mingled with strings of chirrups

White head old birds in the tree likely to recall the Gospel

Old Francis of Azzizzi used to preach to them centuries ago

As if the innocent chirrups were just meant to repeat the

Word——

Repent for sordid things shouldn't have but done anyway

Regretfully repeat again and again and again and again

重覆・懺悔

輾轉反側還是不想起床喔

像瀏覽器發動搜尋的官能拼命要去抓牢

有意義有意思的或者令人高興的什麼

想減輕一點罪惡感吧　不過所犯下所做過的過錯

總也無可奈何不知為何一錯再錯

房間裡產生的一些非比尋常的細細瑣瑣

惱人的地步一如日常家居千篇一律的細瑣

百無聊賴　重覆再重覆的細瑣細瑣

不意從窗外高大的玉蘭樹梢欣喜地傳來

帶著神秘氣息的沙沙風聲　一陣又一陣

那豈不是施洗者約翰在荒野一陣又一陣地

呼叫著懺悔吧　而樹叢的啾啾鳥鳴也在應和呢

白頭翁鳥兒們可都記得古老白髮的聖芳濟

曾向牠們傳福音一遍又一遍　一回又一回呢

那無辜的啾啾鳥鳴無非就是傳道喔──

要為那些明知不該做的　卻無奈地一而再再而三

犯下卑鄙齷齪的行為　一而再再而三地懺悔再懺悔

A Tiny Piece of Heaven

——To my gracious husband

Goodness is 100 percent paradise

A tiny piece of heaven just outside the door

Opening to the balcony dwelling in pot s 99 flowers

All of them are all wives of a man but I——

His only concubine

Every morning and evening I stand

Either inside or outside of the door

Just look with irresistible jealousy at

Their thrilling stunning beauty and

Breathtakingly variety but one thing

We all share more breathtakingly is

What fortitude a husband might endure

To take one more concubine while meddling

With 99 wives envious and shrewd

一片小小的天堂
——送給我的好丈夫

良善是百分之一百的樂土
一片小小的天堂就在開出去的門外
有九十九朵居住在盆景中的陽台
她們都是一個男人的正妻而我

卻是他唯一的小妾
每天清晨以及黃昏
我站在門裡或門外
以無可遏止的妒嫉望著她們的
美麗不得不叫我欣喜欲狂她們的

風情萬種真令人無法置信簡直要人
抓狂然而有一件更加令人無法置信的事
她們卻想要和我一同分享——也就是一個
丈夫該有多大的膽識能耐竟敢弄來一個小妾
當他還得張羅九十九個的正妻個個好妒又精明

輯三　沉默和語言

Part 3 Silence and Language

Soundless Saying of Silence

Since very very young

God has been extremely bright

Being taught what to say

So LIGHT says he and saying

Made him more and more bright

More and more split away from the dark

Being endlessly whirling and falling

Darkness never taught nothing to say

You have to climb blindly the dangerous

Treacherous cliffs just to prevent from

Falling to no bottom

Falling to no saying

Where darkness is the deepest

When we are bound to go through

Our painstakingly climbing would be in vain

Perhaps the more climbing the deeper we

Falling to no bottom

Falling to no saying

Thankfully Psalm twenty-three to read

So what protect and save us from falling is

SAYING of the shepherd's staff and rod

And open a shinning path in the darkness

As the silence dwelling in the heart of Light

The soundless center of Saying extremely bright

沉寂無語的說法

打從很小很小的時候
上帝就絕頂靈光
打從會說話開始
他就說要有光他越說
越靈光也和黑暗分離
越來越遙遠

迴旋不止沉淪無盡
黑暗不會說話也無可言說
你只能在莫名的懸崖峭壁間
驚險萬狀地攀爬翻越怕只怕

跌落至無窮無盡的底部
沉淪至無可言說的地步

當黑暗變成死蔭幽谷
當我們又不得不穿過
我們心驚膽顫無濟於事
甚至於越往上攀爬越向下
跌落至無窮無盡的底部
沉淪至無可言說的地步

真慶幸我們有詩篇二十三可讀
其實守護和救贖我們不至沉落的
是一句耶和華牧者的桿和杖的說法
就能在黑暗中開拓出一條閃亮的路
在沉寂的正中央發出一道光
他的無聲說法卻無限靈光

The Blind Sleeping Little Pig

"I came to this world to judge, so that the blind should see and those who see should become blind"

——*Jesus Christ*

Peeping is unthinkable for the blind
But the blind should see

There's the little thing, she said softly but warned him not to do
But she's sleeping, he replied and just rudely insisted to do
I was the little thing not sleeping and not so little
As less than seven but more than eleven and
Perfectly aware of just what they meant to do

But there seemed some decent authority in her soft voice

I felt my eyelids overwhelmingly pressed by a force

That a little pig must obediently keep its eyes closed as

An innocent little thing and should fall fast asleep

As a little pig being expected and ought to

As long as opening of the eyes absolutely forbidden

In my total blindness I felt so easy and safe

So crystal clear I could not only see with my mind

Free of embarrassment I could also read

The saintly thoughts of their minds

Happened quite unusaul tonight

They had a blind sleeping little pig as a new guest witness

Of their doing things insignificant as domestic bustles

Of any married people and on the other hand

So significant as fatally treacherous

To the realm of Birth of Death and of

ETERNITY

瞎眼睡著的小豬

「我為審判到這世上來，叫盲眼的能看見，能看見
的反瞎了眼」

——耶穌基督

不可能叫瞎眼的偷偷看見
卻可能叫瞎眼的真正看見

有小傢伙在，她輕聲說，其實是不要他做
她睡著了，他答說，不管如何還是要做
我就是那小傢伙　但並沒有睡著　而且也不太小
不是七歲不到而是十一歲有餘
在此關鍵時刻有什麼事要發生
我真是太清楚不過

但她輕柔的語聲裡有一種端莊的威嚴
我的眼皮似乎被一股無可抗拒的力量壓住
使我非得乖順地緊緊閉著雙眼不可
像一個不懂那種事的小傢伙
像一頭真正睡著了的小豬

既然張開眼睛是絕對不許可的
全然的盲瞎反感到輕鬆自在
像水晶般的透徹我不但能一點也不覺得
不好意思地看得清楚　我還能看明白
他們心中的一片聖潔——

今天晚上不比尋常有位新客
一頭瞎眼的睡著了的小豬要來做見證
雖然他們所做的不過是所有已婚者的日用家常
似乎不重要但也重要得沒有比這更生死攸關
更關係著世世代代的
生生不息

The Sound of Turning Key

In an imaginary cage of worry

The crumbs become tasteless even

Drinking water turned oddly bitter

The thought of flight paralyzed the wings

And freedom a word stultifying silly

Although everything suspicious and invisible

Sickness seems the ruthless stark realities on

Either side of the door

Mystery divinity hold the key outside

Inside the soul lost all the senses

Except the big ear attentive only to

The sound of turning the key

Would have nothing to do at all with

The opening of the door and busting out free

But the evidence of no imaginary cage

The prove of no tasteless crumb no paralyzed

Wings no bitter drinking water

No worry no sickness and freedom silly

But only the sound so pleasing and

The key so blessed blissfully turning

扭開鑰匙的聲響

憂慮恍如身在鳥籠

糧粒餅屑的滋味頓失甚至

水喝起來也澀苦無比

想到要飛起來翅膀衹覺癱軟

想到自由這字衹覺再愚蠢不過

令人起疑的那些事雖然看不見

難忍的憂苦總是赤裸裸的現實

存在鳥籠的門裡以及門外

門外那神秘的屬靈者持有鑰匙

門裡那個傢伙已然失去所有官能

衹剩下一隻很大很大的耳朵

專為傾聽是否有扭開鑰匙的聲音
但那聲音無關乎鳥籠的門終於打開
無關乎破門而出自由自在

那是證明根本沒有什麼鳥籠
沒有什麼難嚥的餅屑米糧
沒有癱軟的翅膀沒有澀苦的水
沒有憂慮憂苦沒有愚蠢的自不自由
祇有那正在扭開的屬靈的神鑰
發出欣喜讚頌的聲響

Once by the Bookstore

——To my dearest aunt

Once by the bookstore

I met a very young good woman

She looked at you so lovingly that

You wish you were in one of those eyes

She held your hand so warmly that

You wish you were in one of those palms

She produced a handkerchief from her pockets

To wipe the sweat of hers and yours

You wish you were in one of her pockets

Comfortable easy and safe

As it came to pass she married

She had three children grown up into nothing extraordinary

But you wish you were one of them just the same

And then many a year flowing and flying by

She is getting old very old

I am getting old but not so old

I wish I were in her very oldness all the same

As I indeed believe there is in her very oldness

You can definitely and eventually find

The Word for her so-goodness that I have long failed to find

In all the words all the books in all the bookstores and

The bookstore where I once met her

With a wet handkerchief wiping sweat

From her hands and mine

在那書店的門口
——獻給我最摯愛的阿姨

在那書店的門口

我曾和一個年輕的好女人相遇

她用關愛的眼神望向你

就希望自己從此鑽進她的一隻眼睛裡

她熱呼呼地抓牢你的手

就希望自己從此窩進她的手心

從口袋掏出一條手帕擦你和她自己汗溼的手

就好希望自己從此躲進她衣服的口袋裡

舒適　自在又安全

就這樣過後不久她結了婚

又生了三個小孩長大後祇是平實篤厚的普通人

但不論如何倒希望自己也是其中之一呢

歲月如流時間飛逝她變老而且非常的老

我也變老只是還不如她那麼老

卻希望從此在她的非常的老裡面老

因為我確信在她的非常老的裡面

真的有一個非常好的一個什麼　卻一直找不到

曾在所有的文字裡找不到

曾在所有的書本裡找不到

祇是曾在那書店的門口遇見年輕的她

從口袋掏出一條手帕擦著

我和她自己手中溼溼熱熱的汗

The Legend of 18 Bronze Men

——To my precious daughter

Springs go autumns come and

Flowing by the months and the years

So far away from homeland as my heart

Remorse for a life drifting aimlessly to and fro

Don't you remember the first beautiful song

Your dear father taught when you were

Eighteen months old and you could soon

Pick fully up and sing so amazingly musical

Now that you have finished not only ten

But ten years and eighteen months of

Academic career by the freezing window

Packing and flying homeland almost empty handed

But useless US degrees and one PhD that could

Discourage you but never your mother me

Nor the bravest Eighteen-Bronze-Men melodiously

Singing by the white- head- old birds in the high treetops

Just off the front window of our home you overheard

Every morning when you used to get up early

And never be late and never forget to beckon the dog

Before leaving home for school since you were

Very little but quite a decent scholarly behaved girl

So don't you be discouraged and just off you go

In God we trust and may your father and mother

Me patiently wait and see the accomplishment of

The girl in the legend of 18 bronze men

As reward from Holy God she finally win the

Holy prize that fabricated by Kung Fu mysterious

Sent and sung through white-head-old birds not

For her being able to read and share the thoughts

Of any street dogs by just looking into their eyes

But for her unique talent to translate the chirrups of

White-head-old birds into "Eighteen Bronze Men"

十八銅人的傳奇

——送給我的寶貝女兒

春去秋來

歲月如流

遊子傷飄泊……

還記得爸爸教妳的第一首歌嗎

才十八個月的妳很快就學會

而且從頭到尾唱得一句不漏

還唱得出抑揚頓挫令人叫絕

妳已經完成了不祇十年

寒窗而是十年又十八個月

寒窗研讀的留學生涯

如今匆匆收拾行囊

飛回了家鄉看似一無所獲

只有沒用的美國碩士博士學位

或許妳會覺得氣餒但妳的老媽我

還有那強壯的十八個銅人可都不覺得

且聽那白頭翁的叫聲在高高的樹上

就在我們家前窗外的高樹上那叫聲每天早上

妳總聽得到妳提早起床上學從不遲到

出門前從不忘記和家中的小狗打個面照

記得那時還很小卻有泱泱學者風喔

所以決不可氣餒儘管努力向前行喔

堅信上帝吧且讓妳爸和妳媽

我要耐心地等著瞧等著看

十八銅人傳奇中的那一個女傑

終於榮獲神聖大獎的結局

那是由一種神秘功夫打造而成的獎

並經由白頭翁的鳴聲傳送到人間

這是上帝的賞賜　並非因為觀看狗兒的眼

她就能懂得並分享牠們的心思

而是因為只有她會把白頭翁的啾啾鳴叫

哇貝鐺螂哇貝翻譯成十八銅人十八

So Old So Sweet

The sweetness of being young is illusionary

Becoming old not illusion but a reality starkest

The word "younger" is vaporous and dissolving

But becoming older is definite and steadfast

You can hardly become the youngest

Because the youngest is susceptible to

The most dangerous and lead to annihilation

The oldest tend to be in safe and relief

The bliss of longevity and eternity but Oh

My beloved being so old is not so sweet

Neither is it imaginary illusionary

Just try me and you might feel the strength

Of chewing on the teeth gives you a scent――

The reality of sweetness come real close

老來最美

青春的美不過是一種幻覺
老來面對的是無奈的實在
還很年輕是還在蒸發在溶解
越變越老則是塵埃落定
要變成最年輕是相當不容易的
最年輕最容易遭遇危險
最後不免又是步上毀滅

變成最老倒也安心鬆了口氣
雖說高壽是福祉永生乃喜極
但我的愛啊老來畢竟也不是真的好
並非虛幻一點也不輕飄飄

不過你倒不妨嚐我一口吧感覺我的

勁道我很彈牙會使你產生一種

最甜最美逼近的徵兆

A Drop of Shiny Dew

Nothing desirous but a cheap hotel

Everything cheap but a heart throbbing

A heart throbbing used to laugh at her

What a drop of shiny dew only too salty

Too salty or too watery

No sooner would she become

Weary of him than all be washed

Away into the ocean salty and watery

A radiance come upon the ocean Oh you Romeos

Gracious Sun may give beatitude and retrieve back

Each Juliet of yours' into every drop of dew for you

So sublime and tastes freshly salty as well as watery

一粒閃亮的露珠

沒有什麼更孔急除了一家低廉的旅館
什麼都低廉除了一顆活迸亂跳的心
一顆活迸亂跳的心卻總是笑著說
一粒多麼閃亮的露珠祇是太鹹了點

不論太鹹了點還是太清湯寡水
一旦她對他感到乏味從此所有的一切
全部流散沖刷殆盡流入了大海洋
那既太鹹又清湯寡水的大海洋

當一道美麗的光輝臨照大海洋 羅密歐們啊

喜捨的太陽將降福且從那大海洋

竟然重新撿回你們的每一位茱麗葉在

一粒太鹹又太淡的瑰麗的露珠裡

輯四　遇見最初於未來

Part 4
To Meet the Origin in the Future

Suite One ———————————————————

To Meet the Origin in the Future

"The path not taken is one of the most trodden"

——*Stephen Spender*

From far far away the time future

Swirling around by multifarious words

The Word was calling me by soft and gentle silence

Accompanied sometimes by tender whisperings

Of leaves of laurel fig trees shaking by the wind

So hours and hours of flying in turbulent air

Miles and miles of driving in sloping and twisting roads

I traveled days and nights from the other end of the future

Not only in response of the far far away tender silent calls

But to say last prayers for my daughter's old old car

Now that right at this end of the future I arrived indeed

It is painfully beautiful because when the wind shakes the leaves

Of maple trees by the window of her little gabled house

Making whisperings just as tender as leaves of laurel fig trees by

Mine and perhaps by my 93-yrs-old mother's window in Shanghai

At the other end of the future which is the time origin of us all

If the path never taken is one of the most trodden

Towards the door we never opened into the rose garden

To me the lovely paved path seemed so familiar and reminiscently

Nostalgic as it led to the dooryard of my daughter's gabled little

house

Although I have never trodden on before but perhaps my footfalls

Would soon heard on any path toward any door into the rose

garden no more

Just as any hiss of her old old car unheard nomore

After having accomplished the American dream

By touring and sight-seeing around in it's buckled seats

For every member of the master's family

The day my daughter junked her old old car to the scrap-yard

I prayed bravely tearful that to us this car had been so dedicated

In the time past but the inevitable destiny for both cars and men

Is to meet the origin of ours in the time future

遇見最初於未來

遇見最初於未來

「從未走過的路卻是最常去踩的」

——史蒂芬‧史班德

打從遙遠遙遠的未來時光
雖被千言萬語所縈繞迴旋
「道」以溫文儒雅的沉默
總在不斷地向我召喚著
時而隨伴著風搖動榕樹
葉蔭裡透出悄悄的絮語

極其長時的飛行不斷遭遇大氣的亂流
極其漫長的車程歷經曲折延綿的路途

打從未來的另一頭連日連夜我奔波於旅程

為的不祇是要回應那溫柔而無言的召喚

也是要為女兒的老爺車做最後一次的祈禱

如今我已真正抵達未來時光的這一頭

但有一種很痛楚的美麗是因為她的小樓窗前

風吹楓樹樹葉發出的悄悄絮語和榕樹樹葉在我窗前

甚至在上海的九十三歲母親的窗前所發出的也一樣溫柔

而我們都在未來時序的另一頭那也是我們共同的最初

從未踩過的小徑通向從未開啟的門扉

是意識之中最常去踩去開的因為它

開向我們心識國度之中的玫瑰花園

她屋前草坪間鋪著一條細長美麗的小徑

為何總覺得它如此熟悉令我懷舊感念

雖然說也不記得在它的上面踩過踏過

但隔不多久任何小徑上都聽不到我的跫音

像女兒的那部老爺車載過家裡的每一個人

到處遊歷成全了美國夢終於功成身退
此後再也沒人能夠聽到它絲絲的聲響了

那天就要將老爺車送往廢棄場了
我淚眼盈眶卻鼓起勇氣祈禱著
這部車在過去對我們人類鞠躬盡瘁死而後已
故而遇見最初於未來不論是對車類對人類
都是一種無可迴避的命運喔

Nostalgia for the Things Never have been and Never be

My love is a red red rose

Bloomed in early June and late

In July after years thirty-nine

My love immortal died

Perhaps you are forgetful

Oh my poet my prophet but

Your eyes lighted all my life

And your words said as pure

As gold and there were things of

Graciousness done between us but

So scanty and so still there is

Room spacious for nostalgia

For the things never have been

And never be

懷舊那不曾也不再經歷過的

我的愛是殷紅的玫瑰

盛開在六月初相隔三十九年的

七月末我那永不死的愛死了

或許你並不太記得了但

你是我的詩人我的先知

是你的眼睛點燃了我的人生

對於我你的言談珍貴似純金

我們和樂融融的相處曾經

發生過的事情可以說很少很少

因此我們之間還有寬闊的空間

足夠為那不曾也不再經歷的部份

懷舊

The Final Full Stop

Spring rain came to knock the door of the root

Reluctant to answer the root tend to stubborn

Leaving his ex-wife to talk to the answering machine

Every time when she called and together with

The junk mail he delete all her e-mails to him

Finally she decided to find the root in poetry land

Not interested in all the words the poet yielded

But only the Word from above the Almighty

Not concerned with all the punctuations except

The commas where she could take some air fresh

Skip his fussy question and exclamation marks

Spring rain slip deep into the root of him wherein

Nothing can do but home party of the estranged

A final full embrace in the final full stop of poetry

To the sound of spring rain she made her entry

最後的句點

春雨來敲著草根的門
懶得來應門的草根很是頑固
總叫他的前妻跟答錄機講話
她每次打電話回家還把她所有的
電子郵件當成垃圾郵件一並刪除

前妻決定到詩的園地來找草根
詩人產出的一切字句她無啥興趣
除了出自至高全能者的那個字句
那一些標點符號也多半無關緊要
祇不過來到逗點可以呼吸新鮮空氣

匆匆掠過那無關大局的問號驚嘆號
春雨竟悄悄溜進了草根深深的根
離異的雙方祇得重新開宴來個轟趴
在一首詩的最後句點裡終將相擁
在春雨的激濺喧囂中她踏入家門

Something Real Come Close Sublime

One day when we were young

Not one wonderful morning in May

But one fine afternoon in April

With your quaint smile in dimples

We met and would like to laugh and discuss

Quite often we kiss but sleep only once

Then came the time to part

There you died a virtuoso

Here I lived a veteran of some sort

In between the door ajar

Where ocean and illusion are

Not so soon would ocean be drained

But illusion easily turned into disillusion

Seemingly sneaky and underline

Perhaps illusion is the scent of

Something real come close sublime

真實逼近的絕妙

當時我們青春年少
但那可不是美好的的五月清晨
記得是悠閒的四月午後時光吧
當你的酒窩裡映著精緻的微笑
我們相遇總是那麼愛說說笑笑
不時我們也接吻也上過床一次
然後就來到分手的時候了
在那邊你死了你已是大師

在這裡我活著祇是個老不朽
虛掩的門在我們中間相隔
窄窄的門縫裡卻是海洋與幻覺

那海洋不至於迅速乾涸
但幻覺很快會醒悟破滅成空
鬼鬼祟祟似無還有
或許幻覺是一種徵兆預示著
真實逼近時刻的絕妙

Cookie Store

——To some poets

As I am just a bird flying by

Someone baking cookie from floury snow

Instead of snowy flour

When the earth waits for snow and

The snow waits for the thaw

Some other would sprinkle frost

Instead of sugar on the cookie

When the moonlight shining on the bedside

Seemingly some frost spreading on the floor

And a crooked cook cookie would use

A snake instead of an egg

Even if he should have asked me of

A cock I would not give him such a cookie

All I care is that from all assorted cookie

Might fall upon the shelf and floor of the store

Some real organic crumbs for us

To share with delight in nature

As I am just a bird flying by

糕餅烘焙店
——給一些詩人

我不過是一隻飛過來的小鳥

有人烘焙糕餅是用像麵粉似的白雪

而不是用白雪似的麵粉

當大地總是在等待著白雪

而白雪總也在等待著融解

還有人在小甜餅上面灑的

是霜而不是白糖

有如床前明月光

疑是地上霜的霜

至於那古怪的甜餅烘焙師
他做餅用一條蛇不是一個蛋
要是他問我要一隻公雞
我也不會給他這樣做出來的甜餅

我只關心店裡從那各式各樣的糕餅上
不免掉落在貨架和地面上的碎屑
是否是一些真正的有機的碎屑
讓我們可以像在自然界一樣快樂地分食
因為我不過是一隻飛來的小鳥

A street Named Cool-and-Young

Back and forth our Time travels fatalistically of
Both ends of our Street named Cool- and -Young

Heaven knows since when rancid butter devoured
Cat of our neighbor Miss Jiang lost life and soul and
Vanished in the backyard wilderness of the dormitory
Buildings long deserted for disposal of the realtors
Rain or shine her desperate yelling "Butter...Butter!"
"A kitty with blue ribbon knot and silver bell on the neck"
In the noon time almost often reminiscent of

My dog, when he was at his height like the name of our street

Cool and Young even neighbors calling him Big King Mount

Accustomed to go straight forward to mate

At the other end of our street where a bunch of

Subordinates and concubines gathered around

Quite a span of life for a dog though

He died at age of 9 soon after the passing away of

A 109- year- old veteran soldier neighbors said to have fought

The Revolutionary War in Wu-hang in the other end of Time

That was long after the death of a 59- year- old policeman

Father of an EQ retarded son once lived next door of the same

Old dormitory building that now turned lifelessly empty

Dangling hinged doors slapping in the wind howling and whirling

The EQ retarded son would slipped into the ghostly darkened room

Chatting fervently to some unseen shadows in Shantung dialect mimic

Of his father whose soul always seemed roaming homelessly

Traveled a long long way from the other end of Time

And alas upon the lips of his offspring dwelled frantically

What I presume is the fate of the souls of two grade school boys

Killed in traffic accident 30 years ago at the other end of Street

No sooner had their souls fled to this end of Street Cool-and-Young

Than they turned vivid alive making chirrups of White-head-old

Birds in high Yulan tree tops not far away from my front window

On the windowsill lily petals in pot seeming to be

Patted by the tail invisible of my dog's soul

Substitute for swaggering of it in a way pleasing me so

When he was once Cool and Young used to mate at

The other end of Street and now his loyal soul for sure

Has fled back fatalistically to this end of our time Future

一條街的名字叫昆陽

穿梭於我們宿命的時代的兩端如同往返
我們昆〔Cool-and-〕陽〔Young〕街的兩頭

天知道鄰居江小姐吞噬了變味黃油的貓咪
到底是何時一命嗚呼從此消逝於那一排老舊
宿舍後院的荒煙漫草之中的　　這裡早就是一片
廢棄久矣祇等仲介業者來處置買賣的房產了
陰晴不論風雨無阻她總是呼喊著　　奶油啊奶油
看到那個貓咪嗎　　脖子掛有銀色鈴噹
繫在藍絲帶蝴蝶結上

聽到她的呼叫經常在中午時分

不免思念起我養過的那條公狗

牠年輕氣盛就像我們這條街叫昆陽

又酷Cool-and-又Young鄰居們公認牠為

山大王因為牠總愛直奔街的另一頭尋配

那是牠的地盤總有一批隨扈一群侍妾

就狗兒來說九歲算是長壽了

牠死的那年那位一百零九歲的元老級戰士

剛辭世不久鄰居們說他曾參加武漢革命打過仗

那是時代的另一端的種種事蹟了

狗死的多年前住在他隔鄰死了一位五十九歲

警察他心智不足的問題兒子都曾住在那一長排

老宿舍區現在變成了廢墟了無人氣

晃盪不止的門板斜掛在門框鉸鍊上

打旋的晚風呼嘯著

劈哩啪拉地拍響著

心智不足的問題兒子溜進鬼氣森森的屋內口沫橫飛

滔滔不絕對著鬼魂魅影講一口山東土話的口氣
就跟他老爸一模一樣或許那無株可棲的老靈魂
多少年來四處飄忽終於從時光的那一頭飄來這一頭
好不容易找到了自己的後生晚輩心智不足
說好說歹不知怎地就祇好在他嘴巴上留駐

三十年前在街那一頭因車禍喪身的
兩名小學生的靈魂的命運又如何
想來這一對幼小靈魂從昆陽街那端
飄到這端隔不多久就變成高大玉蘭樹
樹梢白頭翁短啼長鳴的啾啾叫聲了
那棵高大的玉蘭樹離我居家的窗前不遠

窗台上盆栽百合花的花瓣被那一條
看不見的狗的靈魂的尾巴輕輕地拍著
替代牠生前為了討好主人而大搖其尾巴
想當年那又酷Cool-and-又Young 的牠
總是愛跑向昆陽街的那一端去尋配的牠
從未來時光的另一端飄回的是那宿命的忠魂

Old Man, Oh Sea!

By the scenic coast I came to visit you

My beloved but why you greet me

With wind weary and sand sour

Born tender to understand what is love

Born loving to lead the way to forgiving

A secluded room in the lowest layer of

The rocky sediment where I wish

To stay with my beloved overnight

Without conversing kissing embracing

Exchanging fluids with you old man oh sea

To help you button up your shirt one by
One is all I cherished to do the very first thing
In the morning but before wake you up darling
By your silver-shinny face with charming wrinkles
Over the fire dancing against the quaint rocky stove

Let me make breakfast for my beloved old sea
Wait patiently a Sunset- up egg sizzling in pan
Turning from yellow young to golden well-done
The process is perpetual way to eternity
So love turning to forgive as our destiny

老人啊海！

在這美麗的海岸我來看你了
你啊我的愛人卻為何迎接我
以煩人的風　以刺痛的沙
生而溫柔所以懂得如何愛人
生而慈悲所以懂得寬恕之道

在沉積岩的最底層的一間密室
多麼想要和你共度一個夜晚
不必交談無需相吻相擁
更無需交換體液　祇不過
想和你一起共處老人啊海！

天亮起床後我最想做的第一件事
就是幫你把襯衫上一粒
又一粒的鈕扣妥貼扣好　在叫醒你之前
銀亮的臉旁滿滿泛浮的溫柔好看的皺紋
浪花跳舞火燄湧起就著奇岩天成的灶爐

讓我為海為愛做一頓早餐但必須
耐心等候煎在鍋中的荷包蛋它落日朝上
它從青澀的嫩黃漸變成為熟透的金黃
過程是永無止盡到達永恆的永無
止盡無止盡是到達寬恕是慈悲的宿命

結語

　　本書的書名《遇見最初於未來／To Meet the Origin in the Future》乃源自海德格在一篇就語言問題與日本學者研討的對談錄之中，海德格說：「如果當初沒修習過神學作為我的背景，我根本不可能踏上思想研究的這一條路，然而，最初總是打從未來和我們相遇。」

　　海德格對語言問題別具一格探究的深度和廣度，大大影響了我的思維和創作以外，從美國入籍英國，中年以來又篤信基督的英詩泰斗艾略特的詩作及其至為精闢的詩論，尤其在「道（Word）」與「字（word）」，宗教與審美以及時間與意識之間的關照論述與辯證，令人折服之至因而激發出我不少的創作靈感，在所難免也。至於那承載了神的話語的書中之書──《聖經》，對我整體創作生活上的啟迪、激勵、鞭策和引領更在前述思想家與大詩人，以及在其它所有一切文學藝術與思想著作之上，實乃無需贅言矣。

國家圖書館出版品預行編目

遇見最初於未來：硯香詩集 = To meet the
origin in the future / 硯香作. -- 一版.
-- 臺北市：秀威資訊科技, 2009. 12
面； 公分. --（語言文學類；PG0321）

BOD版
ISBN 978-986-221-382-7（平裝）

851.486 98023936

 語言文學類 PG0321

遇見最初於未來──硯香詩集

作　　　者/硯　香
發　行　人/宋政坤
執　行　編　輯/胡珮蘭
圖　文　排　版/鄭維心
封　面　設　計/陳佩蓉
數　位　轉　譯/徐真玉　沈裕閔
圖　書　銷　售/林怡君
法　律　顧　問/毛國樑　律師
出　版　印　製/秀威資訊科技股份有限公司
　　　　　　　台北市內湖區瑞光路583巷25號1樓
　　　　　　　電話：02-2657-9211　傳真：02-2657-9106
　　　　　　　E-mail：service@showwe.com.tw
經　　銷　　商/紅螞蟻圖書有限公司
　　　　　　　台北市內湖區舊宗路二段121巷28、32號4樓
　　　　　　　電話：02-2795-3656　傳真：02-2795-4100
　　　　　　　http://www.e-redant.com

2009 年 12 月　BOD 一版　財團法人│國家文化藝術│基金會 贊助出版
定價：190 元　　　　　　　National Culture and Arts Foundation

讀　者　回　函　卡

感謝您購買本書，為提升服務品質，煩請填寫以下問卷，收到您的寶貴意見後，我們會仔細收藏記錄並回贈紀念品，謝謝！

1.您購買的書名：＿＿＿＿＿＿＿＿＿＿＿＿＿＿＿＿＿

2.您從何得知本書的消息？

　□網路書店　□部落格　□資料庫搜尋　□書訊　□電子報　□書店

　□平面媒體　□ 朋友推薦　□網站推薦　□其他＿＿＿＿＿

3.您對本書的評價：(請填代號　1.非常滿意 2.滿意 3.尚可 4.再改進)

　封面設計＿＿　版面編排＿＿　內容＿＿　文/譯筆＿＿　價格＿＿

4.讀完書後您覺得：

　□很有收獲　□有收獲　□收獲不多　□沒收獲

5.您會推薦本書給朋友嗎？

　□會　□不會，為什麼？＿＿＿＿＿＿＿＿＿＿＿＿＿＿＿＿

6.其他寶貴的意見：＿＿＿＿＿＿＿＿＿＿＿＿＿＿＿＿＿＿

　＿＿＿＿＿＿＿＿＿＿＿＿＿＿＿＿＿＿＿＿＿＿＿＿＿＿

　＿＿＿＿＿＿＿＿＿＿＿＿＿＿＿＿＿＿＿＿＿＿＿＿＿＿

　＿＿＿＿＿＿＿＿＿＿＿＿＿＿＿＿＿＿＿＿＿＿＿＿＿＿

讀者基本資料

姓名：＿＿＿＿＿＿＿＿＿　年齡：＿＿＿　性別：□女 □男

聯絡電話：＿＿＿＿＿＿＿　E-mail：＿＿＿＿＿＿＿＿＿

地址：＿＿＿＿＿＿＿＿＿＿＿＿＿＿＿＿＿＿＿＿＿＿＿

學歷：□高中(含)以下　　□高中　　□專科學校　□大學

　　　□研究所(含)以上 □其他＿＿＿＿＿＿＿

職業：□製造業 □金融業 □資訊業 □軍警 □傳播業 □自由業

　　　□服務業 □公務員 □教職　□學生 □其他＿＿＿＿＿

(請沿線對摺寄回,謝謝!)

秀威與 BOD

BOD（Books On Demand）是數位出版的大趨勢，秀威資訊率先運用 POD 數位印刷設備來生產書籍，並提供作者全程數位出版服務，致使書籍產銷零庫存，知識傳承不絕版，目前已開闢以下書系：

一、BOD 學術著作—專業論述的閱讀延伸
二、BOD 個人著作—分享生命的心路歷程
三、BOD 旅遊著作—個人深度旅遊文學創作
四、BOD 大陸學者—大陸專業學者學術出版
五、POD 獨家經銷—數位產製的代發行書籍

BOD 秀威網路書店：www.showwe.com.tw
政府出版品網路書店：www.govbooks.com.tw

　　永不絕版的故事・自己寫・永不休止的音符・自己唱